To:

_____

From:

_____

PRAYERS
ON
MY PILLOW

PRAYERS
ON
MY PILLOW

Inspiration for girls
on the threshold of change

CELIA STRAUS

BALLANTINE BOOKS • NEW YORK

A Ballantine Book
Published by The Ballantine Publishing Group

Copyright © 1998 by Celia Straus
Introduction copyright © 1998 by Julia Straus

http://www.randomhouse.com

Library of Congress Cataloging-in-Publication Data

Straus, Celia.
    Prayers on my pillow : inspiration for girls on the threshold of
  change / Celia Straus. — 1st ed.
      p.   cm.
    Summary: A compilation of nondenominational prayers loosely
  organized into sixteen sections or categories addressing specific
  issues or problems of teenage girls.
    ISBN 0-345-42673-8 (alk. paper)
    1. Teenage girls. — Prayer books and devotions — English.
  [1. Teenage girls.   2. Prayer books and devotions.]   I. Title.
  BL625.9.T44S77   1998
  291.4'33'08352 — dc21   98-21643
                                                            CIP

Book design by H. Roberts Design
Cover design by Min Choi

Manufactured in the United States of America

First Edition: November 1998
10 9 8 7

For my girls, Julia and Emily, and for girls everywhere.

Contents

Acknowledgments

These prayers were written out of love for my daughters. However, I would not have been able to offer them to other girls without the help of Cherie Burns, my friend and literary agent, who first saw them as a book and Joanne Wyckoff, my wise and wonderful editor at Ballantine, who brought them to publication. I also wish to thank the following for their help and encouragement: Caroline Bain, Josh Baran, my father, Ray Brim, Katherine Brim, Susan Piver Browne, Linda Chambers, Melinda Curly, Chaplain Norm Folkers, Chris Jones, Erika Leiberman, Father Berard Marthaler, Reverend Sandra Mayo, Toby and Carol Marquez, Kathy McGloughlin, Shannon Mizell, Maggie Petito, Dennis Reeder, Irina Reyn, Tina Salvesen, Paula Silver, Charyn D. Sutton, Reverend Elizabeth Orens and Reverend Amy Yount of the National Cathedral School, and all those girls and mothers who read and responded to the prayers as this book was being compiled. Most of all, for making this book—and my family—complete, I am grateful to my husband, Richard. Finally, as a daughter, I thank my mother, Patricia Brim, for she, too, answered prayers.

PRAYERS
ON
MY PILLOW

Why I Wrote the Prayers

Prayers on My Pillow was written for my older daughter, Julia. I started writing the prayers in the fall of 1995, when, at age twelve, Julia began experiencing many of the physical and emotional changes of young adolescence. A brave, happy, independent, and outgoing girl was fast becoming vulnerable, confused, and withdrawn right before my eyes. At the same time, as a self-employed writer for television, I was carrying a heavy workload. It seemed that, as the days went by, there was less and less time to talk with Julia, and more and more need to do so.

There also seemed to be new barriers to overcome every time we *did* talk. Suddenly my previously valued and much sought after opinions, observations, witticisms, and advice were off-base, outdated, and boring. Suddenly I wasn't listening properly, was hopelessly "out of it," or "didn't understand." And Julia, who up until now had been forthcoming and honest about what she was feeling, began responding to my inquiries with a "whatever" or a silent shrug of the shoulders.

We'd had a tough summer. Julia had found few friends to hang out with at the beach, so she had spent most of her time alone. Then she and I were in a frightening car accident in which the car was totaled, though neither of us was hurt. We both realized our mortality at the same moment, and the realization stayed with us. I think we also both realized that our relationship, built on communication that was continual and close, one that had nurtured and supported Julia throughout her young life, was changing. The connections between us were breaking down. Even more important, the connections within Julia herself were breaking down. Because of numerous factors including age, sex, society, school, and the accelerated pace of life in the nineties, Julia's sense of self, her very essence, was threatened.

As I think back, it was Julia who asked me to write the first prayer. We're not a particularly religious family. I'm Christian, brought up Episcopalian, and my husband is Jewish. Like many interfaith couples who marry and have children, we dealt with our religious differences by pretty much avoiding the topic entirely. Not going to church or synagogue. Celebrations of Christmas and Passover focused on secular rituals and family traditions, and observance of Easter, Yom Kippur, or Rosh Hashanah was nonexistent.

I had taught Julia and her younger sister, Emily, one bedtime prayer—the only one I ever prayed when I was a child. It's from a 1920 children's book called *The Bam Bam Clock*, by J. P. McEvoy. It goes like this:

> Bless me, God, the long night through,
> And bless my mommy and daddy, too,
> And everyone who needs Your care,
> Make tomorrow bright and fair,

And thank You, God, I humbly pray,
For all You did for me today.

It did the job for ten years. But during that busy, tumultuous autumn, when I was preoccupied with work and Julia's troubles were mounting, she asked me to write her a new one. One that might help her go to sleep instead of staying up until one or two in the morning worrying about . . . well, everything.

And so I did. The next day I wrote a prayer, in verse. I'm not a scholar of religion or a person "of the cloth." I believe in an Infinite Being whom I call God, an afterlife, and the power of prayer. I'm not a poet. I write television dramas, documentaries, and educational videos. Occasionally, I've worked on a novel. But I do know the profound difference between writing from the head and writing from the heart. This first prayer and all the hundreds after it came from the heart. And that night I put the first prayer on Julia's pillow.

Each day thereafter, whether we had had a chance to talk or not, I wrote a prayer for her to pray before she went to bed. Sometimes we read them together, sometimes she read them by herself, sometimes we talked about them. And I learned how important they were to her when, one night when I didn't write one, she asked me where her prayer was. I was careful to write the prayers in the words and voice that she might have chosen for herself. Some were tools to help her handle crises in her life; others were written as celebrations of her victories. Some were meditations on life cycles and the importance of acting in faith and love; others were more lighthearted and emphasized perspective and balance in order to get beyond the intense self-absorption of her adolescence.

I wrote the prayers having been deeply impressed by Mary Pipher's *Reviving Ophelia* and Peggy Orenstein's *School Girls*, books that stressed the need for parents to maintain connections with daughters during the early years of adolescence. I was also inspired by Larry Dossey's book *Healing Words: The Power of Prayer and the Practice of Medicine*, all of Max Freedom Long's books about Huna, especially *Growing into Light*, Enid Hoffman's *Huna, a Beginner's Guide,* Thomas Moore's *Care of the Soul*, and the writings of Reverend Sandra Mayo.

The prayers are nondenominational and are based on a very basic three-part concept. First, they acknowledge the existence of an Infinite Deity or Absolute Being, who is addressed as either God or Lord. Second, they look at life from the perspective of the girl who is praying. And third, they acknowledge and respect the girl's inner self, or soul. Each prayer then connects and integrates the three. The process is simple and powerful. In the three-part concept there is a replacement of negative feelings or thoughts with a positive act of faith.

No matter what life issue a prayer addresses— a problem to be solved, an anticipated challenge, gratitude, celebration, awareness of the beauty of nature, despair, loneliness, boredom—the process is the same. An experience or perception of a young teenage girl along with her ensuing emotions is recognized and then put into the context of, or sandwiched between, Inner Self and God.

Within that loving and secure framework, the prayers gently remind the reader of what she is capable. They present truths and values she can trust and rely on, such as fearless faith, love, self-reliance, self-empowerment, and ethical behavior.

Many also express the benefits of courage, generosity, humor, creativity, and risk taking.

The prayers are *not* guilt-based. The word *guilt* is never used. Neither are they requests for what most people pray for—world peace, good health, better grades, career success, or material goods. The prayers are not whiny or self-pitying. They encourage girls to look inward rather than outward for the strength to solve their problems. As a result, they help girls discover and tap their inner strengths to cope with changes.

The prayers are written in verse rather than prose, not because they are poems, but simply because that makes them easier to remember. They are practical, hands-on tools, like a makeup brush or a hammer, except they are tools of the spirit. They are to be used as very private, very personal, and very loving Acts of Faith. They work magic because they tap into our own spiritual energy, which is as real and powerful as gravity and exists in all of us whether we acknowledge it or not.

The prayers are loosely organized into sixteen sections or categories addressing different reasons for girls to pray. There's a prayer on each page because

7

both Julia and I found that praying one new prayer each night was more than enough to think about. Not all prayers will prove useful to every reader. However, certain ones will strike an instant chord and become favorites. And a few of those can become crucial for handling day-to-day events.

Each prayer—or, for that matter, any word or combination of words within each prayer—can be used as a mantra, affirmation, meditation, thought, chant, song, or daily reminder, either expressed out loud or not. The prayers are completely flexible. They can and should be copied out and personalized by the girls who read them. They can and should be wadded up into small squares and kept in a wallet, backpack, jewelry box, notebook, diary, or locket. There is space in this book to write new prayers tailored to meet the different and new needs of each reader.

I believe the prayers have made a positive difference for both Julia and Emily. One indication is that both girls agreed to share these deeply personal prayers with other girls. I would like to think that this demonstration of their glorious inner strength and generosity of spirit was enhanced by my efforts, but then I can hardly be objective about my daughters. I am, however, deeply grateful for their existence and the opportunity I have been given by God to write prayers for them—and you.

—Celia Straus

Why the Prayers Have Meant So Much to Me

My mom and I have always been close. Ever since I was little, we have been able to talk, and I have felt that I could come to her with my problems. That's not to say we don't have our differences. I would be the first to admit that we quarrel and get on each other's nerves like most mothers and daughters. But I feel that I am closer to my mom than most girls are to their mothers. That is why, a couple of years ago, it upset me so much that we never had time to talk— particularly when there seemed to be so many more things, problems, changes to discuss. Every day we would say we would talk that night, yet every night we were both too tired. When I came home from school, she was working. Later in the evening I was doing homework, or on the phone or in the shower. Although we still saw each other all the time, it felt like we hadn't talked, alone, together for a long time.

So one day I asked her to write something for me. I knew she was a wonderful writer, so I asked her to write a prayer. Nothing long or fancy, just a simple form of communication. That night I found a folded piece of paper on my pillow. On it was a short prayer she had typed on the computer. I immediately fell in love with the idea. So every day Mom would write a prayer, and every night I would read it. If it was a holiday, or I had a big test, or a sports game, the prayer would address that subject. Sometimes Mom would come and read them to me. I felt like a little kid being read a book, but the book was written just for me.

The prayers gave me something to look forward to. Not only did they address typical "teenage problems," but they also were like a kiss goodnight. I would read some over and over again to remember certain lines. But my favorite part was having a different prayer every day. There were so many to choose from. It was not at all like recalling the same prayer over and over again until it had lost all its meaning. There was a new and different meaning every day.

I must admit that initially I was not crazy about the idea of the prayers being made into a book. I thought that they were something special between just my mom and me. But as I showed them to some of my friends, I realized that others could benefit from them also. Other girls have the same problems and questions that I have. Now I am glad that others will have the opportunity to share in these prayers. I hope that they will help other girls the way they have helped me.

—Julia Straus

THE COURAGE
TO BE
MYSELF

I surround myself with toys at night
Just like a little child,
And yet my dreams are different now
With yearnings to be wild.

I pray to keep these two selves safe
Each night before I sleep—
The child in me protected by
The grown-up I'll soon meet.

It's hard to close my eyes sometimes
When deepest needs collide,
The search for self continues strong—
It pulls me like the tide.

Put prayers on my pillow, please,
So I can tread the night
And wake up as the girl I am
To greet, with joy, the light.

There is only one way to have courage,
There is only one way to live,
And that is to find
The self that is mine—
To touch it, to grow it, to make it divine.

There is only one way to battle despair,
There is only one way to win,
And that is to clasp
Each day as my last—
Treasure it, live it, and hold it so fast.

There is only one way to find happiness,
There is only one way to hope,
And that is with faith
That my soul is a place
Where love everlasting comes with God's grace.

As I go through this day
Let me be strong,
Let me believe
That I belong,
Let me build courage
To face down my fears
And replace them with faith
That I'm worth all my tears.
For the self that I value
Is what keeps me great
And makes me the master
Whatever my fate.

Lord, guide me on the journey I make,
For there are different roads to take—
Four-lane highways, smooth and fast,
Filled with people going past.
I could choose those roads and go
With the crowd and never know

A smaller winding road that runs
Counter to the bigger ones
With ruts and hills, not smoothly paved,
Demanding I be strong and brave
But giving me the chance to be
All that You intend for me.

May my angels protect me,
May they hear what I pray,
May they touch oh so gently
As I go through each day.
Let them guide me with secrets
That only I hear
As they lovingly whisper,
"You have nothing to fear."

I pray as I grow older
My spirit will stay strong,
Not weakened by the need to lie
And cover up what's wrong.

I pray as I grow older
My spirit will stay free,
Not trapped by webs of pretense
From fears I can't be me.

I pray as I grow older
My spirit will stay true,
Not twisted into knots of doubt
But certain through and through.

I pray as I grow older
My spirit will stay wild,
Not cowered by the world's demands—
Still proud to be a child.

I pray for connection
Between what I do
And what I feel—
No more relying on
Familiar patterns,
Robotic actions,
To separate me
From emotions,
No going through the motions
Endlessly.

I pray for transition
From false responses
To an honest answer—
No more fear of
Anger and rejection
But risking consequences
To build the bridge
Connecting
What I feel
To what I do.

I am God's child—I am innocent.
I am God's creation—I am beautiful.
I am God's gift—I am generous.
I am God's hope—I am faithful.
I am God's wisdom—I am knowing.
I am God's laughter—I am joyful.
I am God's love—I am me.

May I always be able to run to
That deep place that awaits my return,
Where calm light shines on forever
And there's nothing left for me to learn.

May I go there whenever I need to,
May the door always open at will
As my soul rises up to embrace me
And my mind becomes blessedly still.

As a girl I found the place easy
To hide in and stay there to play.
Now getting back seems to be harder,
Yet I need that place more every day.

I must never lose the way back there—
Inside myself, let me make time
To seek out the light where my soul is,
The place where I'll find what is mine.

Let me know that I have to make choices
Whenever decisions demand.
Let me follow God's truth as I know it,
Use my courage to make a brave stand.

I pray I'll be strong for this choosing,
Especially when choosing is hard.
I pray I'll take time to be thoughtful,
For I don't want my life to be scarred.

And as I consider my options
May I draw on the essence of me:
For the choices I make that are fearless
Are the ones that will keep my soul free.

BRAVE
BEGINNINGS

I pray I can get through this first time—
This first time is what today's for.
As a child I was burdened with first times
But it seems like this year there are more.

I pray for the faith to be certain
That I will appear brave and strong;
Though my stomach's in knots and I'm frightened,
I will trust that this day won't go wrong.

I pray I can handle this first time
So that it becomes the first step
To a better and stronger tomorrow
And the fears of today I'll forget.

My stomach's clenched tight, my nails are chewed.
My face is in blotches, my self's come unglued.
I can't seem to think, I don't know what to say—
I'm confused and embarrassed throughout every day.

I worry about worrying, I feel guilty and fret
About what to remember that I'm sure I'll forget.
I know I'm not perfect; I'm scared I will fail—
When I'm faced with a change, my fears will prevail.

I know I've just started another school year—
But how can I get through each day without fear?
I need to find someplace where I can just be
Alone with my thoughts and the self that is me.

I pray I will be happy
To start another year
As summer ends and summer friends
Begin to disappear.

I pray I will be able
To handle what they ask
Of me in school and yet keep cool
When I can't do the task.

I pray I will be ready
To face my friends again
If they have changed and rearranged
What friendship means to them.

I pray I will be eager
To try what's hard and new
And not lose sight of my soul's right
To shine through what I do.

There is so much to remember to get through the day—
Places to be and new games to play,
Endless details of things I must take
To school and from school, to turn in, to make.
I keep on forgetting where I ought to be
Or who I am when I'm supposed to be me.
I pray I can find just one moment to stop
Remembering things for a person I'm not.

Where is my balance
For this new tightrope?
I've stepped away from childhood
To walk without a net—
Teetering on tiptoe,
Determined to cross
Above the ordinary world
To my own.

Where is my balance
For this high-wire act?
I'm caught in the middle
Taking one step at a time—
Risking my soul,
Determined not to fall,
As my audience waits
Breathless.

Where is my balance
For this aerial ballet?
I stretch out my hands—
Holding faith tight,
Trusting God will guide me,

Determined to leap
Onto the platform
Courage made.

May I be proud
Of how I've lived
For these few years.
I've known some truths,
I've taken risks,
I've chosen paths
That forked and turned
And took me places where I learned
About myself
And others, too,
And how each day brings
Something new.

May I be proud
Of how I look.
As I start out
I've gained some strength,
I've added grace,
My body's changed
In weight and height,
And though it's not exactly right

I like the image
That I see—
The natural universe
In me.

May I start each day
Knowing I can
Take a risk
Though risks may fail,
Dare to dream
What seems absurd,
Shout the truth
When faced with lies,
Choose what's hard
If hard is right,
Fight to win
A noble cause,
Believe in love
Midst those who hate,
Trust in God
To keep me safe.

Thank you, God, for new beginnings.
Starting over gives me hope—
Changing directions,
Finding chances
To reconsider, then try again.

Thank you, God, for resolutions,
Recommitments to improve—
Just the promise to do better
Gives me faith
That I'll succeed.

LOOKING IN
THE MIRROR

When I look in the mirror
And I see myself changed,
With pimples and glasses and teeth ill-arranged,
Let me have faith that this phase will soon pass.
I'll change as I grow—
This me's not the last.

When I cry on my pillow
Hot tears through the night,
Tossing and turning and mourning my plight,
May I remember my problems are small.
In less time than I know
They won't be there at all.

I'm not good to myself
If I hate what is me.
I don't need to punish
The body I see.
God didn't create me
So I'd fade away
By refusing to eat
More than one grape a day.
And yet it is hard
To express what I feel—
I'd rather stay silent,
Skipping a meal.
Controlling myself
In a world so unfair,
I keep very thin
To show that I care.
May I have the strength
To discover the cause,
Instead of reacting
Like I've broken some laws,
And know that my body
Is what houses my soul
And that God will be with me
As I become whole.

My body is the cloak I wear
For this short time on earth,
I can't return this precious gift
That I received at birth.

So let me love each shape and curve
No matter how it looks
Compared to other bodies
In magazines and books.

May I keep it safe from harm,
Prepare it as I grow,
This changing form of energy
Revealing eternal soul.

Whatever I do in this lifetime
Will be done through this body alone.
So let me be proud of its color and shape—
Whatever I have is my own.

Whatever I give to this planet
Will be given through my energy.
So let me be wise in my choices
Of what I take inside of me.

Let me love myself so much
That I never want to hide
The way I think, the way I talk,
My hair, my clothes, the way I walk.

Let me love myself so much
That I'm proud of what I am,
The way I choose to spend my time,
The way I make unique what's mine.

Let me love myself so much
That I never want to change
What I've created through the years
To make me different from my peers.

My face in the mirror is a stranger's—
I can't seem to find myself there.
Please touch me with loving awareness,
Warm my heart so I know that You care.

My soul seems lost and forgotten,
I've strayed off the path I was on.
Please open the door closed behind me,
Lead me back, Lord, to where I belong.

My spirit is longing for comfort,
My eyes search the mirror for clues.
Please show me the way to awareness,
Let me find joy in what is true.

Please help me, God, to see my face,
To find more there than skin and bone,
To see the light reflected back
That tells me I am not alone.

My face seems ugly to me now
With blemishes and shadows deep.
My eyes are worried, my mouth is tight—
It's not a face I'd like to keep.

And yet I force myself to say
It's not today's face that is key
But how my face will change to show
The infinite beauty inside me.

CONFUSION
AND FEAR

Let me stop the war within,
The voices arguing—chaotic din—
Confused by memories they cannot feel
From childhood past no longer real.

Let me find a path to take
Away from pain, away from ache,
Away from endless asking how
That keeps me from the time that's now.

Let me grasp the central knot
That ties me up so I'm still caught
In tangled feelings I can't leave,
In images I can't retrieve.

Let me open one door more
To show me what God's love is for
So I can find the self I know
And finding self, let all pain go.

Please listen to my worry, God,
Please send my worry away.
I've carried it deep inside me, God,
And now it wants to stay.

No matter what I'm doing, God,
It's there, one thought behind.
No matter how forgetful,
It's there for me to find.

Please help me take my worry, God,
To someone who will know
That if I tell them what is wrong
My worry, at last, will go.

When I'm so afraid that I tell a lie,
When I worry one day that my mom will die,
When I feel so sad that I want to cry
But I don't know why, I don't know why . . .
Then, God, please hear my plea.
God, watch over me.

When I think the worst is about to come,
All alone in the house and I hear someone,
When the night falls dark and the light is done
And I want to run, and I want to run . . .
Then, God, please hear my plea.
God, watch over me.

Help me, please, to understand
These feelings of resentment—
No matter what I do or say
I cannot find contentment.

Whatever task is asked of me
I find myself rebelling
As though there's nothing I need do,
For nothing is compelling.

Help me, please, to figure out
Why suddenly I'm screaming
When I must do what I once did
Without this awful seething.

I know I'm not quite in control
Of what's going on inside me.
What can I do to find some peace?
I'm begging You, please guide me.

I worry about death.
It seems so sad:
When people die
They're gone forever
And there's a black hole
Where they used to be.

But I also know
That dying is just a step
In the process of life:
When the body's gone
The soul's still there,
Living in light.

Where can I run
When there's no homeplace left?
Where can I hide
When my parents "know best"?
Who can I turn to
When friends turn me down?
Who can I trust
When there's no one around?
What can I say
When the worst has been said?
What can I feel
When my feelings are dead?
How can I cry
When God's love is right here,
Telling me, "Love,
You have nothing to fear"?

I've just met depression, a friend I can't bear.
It's entered my heart and insists on staying there.
Darkened and solemn, it oftentimes screams,
Sobs through my day hours and blackens my dreams.

Life seems like forever; it's worse than I know.
I feel so awful, each thought is a blow.
I have no defenses, no weapons, no walls
Except what God gives me when God answers my calls.

Please take away the ache inside—
I don't know why the joy has died
But since I woke I've only cried.
The grief is like a rising tide.

I know they'll say I'm far too young
To feel life's ended, not begun—
But that's the way this song is sung.
The innocence I had is done.

Please give me just a sign or clue
That what I feel is not what's true,
And feeling now the way I do
Will be replaced with faith in You.

May I let go of memories
That fill me with pain,
Where I was to blame.
May I release all the memories
That bind me so tight,
That continually fight.
May I dismiss all the memories
That keep me afraid,
That I alone made.
May I throw out the memories—
The ones that are bad,
The ones that are sad.
May I erase all the memories
That use up the time
That could have been mine.
May I keep only the memories
That give me the grace
To move on from this place.

May I find guidance through this maze.
Each day I'm living in a daze,
So confused I cannot take
A single step that isn't fake,
So bewildered by my feelings
That my mind is always reeling.
Stopping, starting, lost in thought,
I cannot find the self I've got—
Tossed and turned by deep emotion,
Filled with conflict and commotion,
Mistakes made with no correction.
Help me, Lord, to find direction.

Before I go to sleep each night,
Before I turn off every light,
Let me put away my fears,
Let me brush away the tears.

Before I start to close my eyes,
Before my dreams begin to rise,
Let me cry my final cry,
Let my stomach's knots untie.

Before I snuggle down in bed,
Before my blankets hide my head,
Let me give myself a gift,
Let my guilty burdens lift.

For I do not deserve to weep
Bitter thoughts before I sleep.
I must believe that God is near
And sleep in peace instead of fear.

FINDING BEAUTY IN MY WORLD

I dance when I wake
To the morning sun
And I dance at night
When the day is done.
I dance to the sounds
Of my running feet
And I dance when I laugh
With the friends I meet.
I dance with myself
And I dance with boys,
And the dance can be quiet
Or make lots of noise.
My dance is God's way
To make joy for me.
I'll dance every day—
For my soul is free.

May I notice Your paintbrush—
How it's touched every tree
With gold and red brush strokes
That are lovely to see.

May I gather Your paint drops
As they're blown to the ground
In patterns of autumn—
Swirling colors abound.

May I praise Your creation—
How You've shaded it all
With oranges and yellows,
Covering summer with fall.

Let me believe in Your magic
That comes with the light—
A world covered in snowflakes,
Quilted deep by the night.

Let me believe in Your magic
That captures my eyes—
A world made of crystals,
Bright morning surprise.

Thank you, God, for endless light.
From the sun's first rays to the soft gray dusk,
I find odd moments to look anew
At familiar places I go each day
And I'm startled by the world I see.
Colors reflected back to me
Are altogether changed each time,
For Nature's way to urge me down
The path I tread and tread again
Must be to light the way so well
That beauty's always there to find.
And with discovery, hope comes, too,
That I will find within myself
That same sweet endless light.

I will kiss the wind
I will rock the sea
I will lift the mountain
I'll caress the tree

I will hold the ground
I will hug the sky
I will love this earth
Until the day I die

When nature starts to grow again,
To mend what winter's torn,
May spring's rebirth take place in me
Each day my soul is born.

When trees bud forth and flowers bloom
And evening sun is warm,
May new strength find a place in me
Each day my soul is born.

When birds build nests and lay their eggs
And sing to greet the morn,
May beauty flourish in my world
Each day my soul is born.

I see You in the sunlight's beams
That chase away my morning dreams.
I see You in the crocus leaves
That peek from underneath the trees.
I see You in the friends I meet
Between my classes, in the street.
I see You in my parents' faces
And in all my secret places.
I see You most when day or night
My mirror reflects Your shining light.

May I dance through June nights
Filled with stars and delights,
May I laugh with sheer joy
That I've found the right boy,
May I dive into pools
Lit to sparkle like jewels,
May I bask in the breeze
Rustling through city trees,
May my soul soar so high
That it touches the sky,
May I thank You above
For this summer of love.

Thank you, Lord, for this silver carpet
Of moonlight
That spreads across my floor
For me to walk on
As I pray.

Thank you, Lord, for evening songs
Of crickets
That fill my summer bedroom,
Keeping me company
As I pray.

Thank you, Lord, for the soft caress
Of ocean breezes
That sweep through my window,
Drying my tears
As I pray.

I am a child of God,
a spirit of the earth,
a part of the universe
from the moment of birth,
a drop of rain
on new green leaves,
a ray of sunlight
filtered through trees,
a bird's soft feather
carried by the breeze,
a clear ice crystal
after a freeze.
In all nature's beauty
I look for my soul
And find it reflected
As part of the whole.

THE PAIN OF
GROWING UP

Today I woke up empty,
My soul completely flown—
As if my self had lost its way,
My song had lost its tone.

Today I woke up numbed inside,
My feelings paralyzed—
As if my mind had given up
The light inside my eyes.

Today I woke dead-ended,
With no place else to go—
As if my life had come full stop
With nothing left to know.

Today I woke no little girl
But someone not yet here—
As if I'd lost the faith to grow
In God instead of fear.

Why am I so impatient, Lord?
Why can't I live for today?
Why do I always wish for tomorrow?
Why do my dreams fade away?

Why am I so unhappy, Lord?
Why can't I like myself here?
Why do I try to be someone I'm not?
Why do I find things to fear?

I am a girl who is waiting, Lord,
Hoping to find who I'll be.
Help me to welcome each moment,
Show me the way to be free.

May I cherish the joy deep inside me,
May I nourish the love there that grows.
May I keep close and safe my unshaken faith
That God always watches and knows.

May I build on the strength deep inside me,
May I treasure my sweet silly side.
May I trust what I feel, for my feelings are real
And my prayers will not be denied.

Dear God, protect my wildish self
Who runs against the tide,
Who reaches up to touch the sky
And dares to dream that she can fly.

Dear God, protect my secret self
Who whispers soft and near,
Creating gifts of inner light
That show the way through darkest night.

Dear God, protect my childlike self
Who sings a joyful song,
Reminding me that I must pray
For sparkling moments every day.

I cannot make them understand,
I cannot make them listen
To how I feel but dare not say
Because I am the one who'll pay
A price if they don't see my way.

I cannot make them sympathize,
I cannot make them care.
Instead I'll be a girl who sees
The self inside and who believes
The silent victories she achieves.

Please help me to judge
What's important, what's not,
To change what I can
In the time that I've got.

Please help me to choose
What's best for my life
Today and tomorrow
Without all the strife.

Please help me to learn
How to take a step back
To see my world clearly
To know how to act.

Please help me to trust
That my instincts are true
And use what I feel
To guide what I do.

I pray that I can always hear
The voice of my self calling, calling,
Urging me to trust my instincts,
Telling me to banish fear.

I pray that I will always say,
My self, listen, my self, listen,
As I tell you what I need,
Ask for strength throughout each day.

I pray that I will always know
Of God's presence deep inside,
The link between my self and soul
Getting stronger as I grow.

I'm adrift in a sea of longings,
Inexpressibly strong.
Tide-timeless feelings
Lift me up
Then toss me aground.

I'm drowning in a sea of wanting
For life to begin.
Deep yearning pools
Pull me down
To their depths.

I'm clinging to a net of prayers
Tangled by faith,
Words woven pleadingly
For God
To save me.

In these few years
I've learned to trust,
I've learned to hope,
I've learned I must
Believe in me
The whole day through—
From dawn to dusk
I must be true.

I define myself with words
Of beauty and strength.
I show myself with acts
Of grace and courage.
I humor myself with smiles
Of silliness and joy.
I guide myself with dreams
Of greatness and fancy.
I soothe myself with whispers
Of caring and healing.
I treat myself with hopes
Of happiness and winning.
I grow myself with love
Of God and Spirit.

PRESSURES IN SCHOOL

When I don't understand what I've set out to do,
I pray to be patient and think it all through
And not just start out as if I alone knew,
When deep down inside I haven't a clue.

When I've missed an assignment or haven't been there,
I pray I won't whine that my life isn't fair
But do what it takes to show that I care
By calling a friend who is willing to share.

When I haven't been told just how to proceed,
I pray I will find one person to lead,
For asking good questions is planting the seeds
To grow gardens of learning instead of just weeds.

God, let me trust that in my brain
I have everything I need
To figure out the numbers game
Or understand the books I read.

God, let me know that I am smart
And powerful inside my mind.
No need to cry or worry—
I can think things out just fine.

God, let me say that I can do it
Every time I fear I'm dumb—
Just one small prayer to keep me going
Until the answers come.

When I can't figure it out,
When I don't know the words,
When the help isn't there,
And my cry isn't heard,

When the numbers don't add
And the notes are not right
And I start feeling scared
That I'm not very bright,

Then let me breathe deeply,
Stop fretting and say,
I know I can do this
If I take time to pray.

It seems, quite often, there's not time,
My life seems squeezed between the lines—
A puppet moved from class to class
With breaks to rest that never last.

Please let me keep in mind the pace
Of God and not attempt to race
So I see time I thought was gone
As coming back just like the dawn.

Frustration
Fills my eyes with tears
Because I just can't
Get it right:
The word misspelled,
The problem wrong,
The smudge I can't erase,
The ball thrown wide,
The tangle tight,
The pimple on my face.

Frustration
Makes me want to scream
And tear the paper
Into shreds.
But let me stop
And take a breath
And pray that I calm down
To find a way
From deep inside
Where answers can be found.

I can do this I know
I can make myself go
I can keep on through pain
I can work 'til I gain
I can weep but then smile
I can rest for a while
I can rise from defeat
I can retake my seat
I can overcome odds
I can pray to my gods
I can win victories
I can use all of me

Whenever I'm waiting for something to happen—
A phone call, a test score, the results to begin—
May I have the wisdom to put my mind elsewhere,
To trust what God brings and calmly give in.

Whenever my stomach is knotted and anxious
With anticipation that won't go away,
May I substitute patience for worry and fretting
And not allow waiting to ruin my day.

Whenever the outcome is all that I care for
And what I went through no longer means much,
Let me remember the joy of the effort,
The moments that show me God's touch.

Why am I never caught up, God?
Why is there not enough time?
No matter the lists, the plans, and the help,
I can't cross that last finish line.

Please give me calm to start over,
The strength to not panic inside,
The faith that all things will work out,
The trust that You'll be there to guide.

In the midst of my lists of place names and facts,
And chapters and stories and cards in their packs,
Please let me learn all I must for each test
And not lose my balance or forget I need rest.

As I memorize, theorize all through the day,
Thumb through my books, notes in full disarray,
Please let me focus on critical things
So I'll know what I should when the testing begins.

And if I get tired and edgy and sad
And fearful this grade is doomed to be bad,
Please let me have confidence, faith, and the hope
That no matter what happens, I'll be able to cope.

Please give me the time to learn what I need to
As I read and study and plan.
Please give me the knowledge to do what I have to
As I solve all the problems I can.

Please grant me the wisdom to stop when I must,
As my eyes start to blur and my head starts to ache.
Please grant me the calm to know I can trust
Just how much my body can take.

And as hours go by when I'm feeling alone,
Please be by my side as I seek
To find understanding in the pages I roam
Of how to be strong for the week.

As I study and study, night after night,
Praying I'll be smart and my thoughts will be bright,
Repeating each date and reciting each word,
Let me give myself grace so my soul will be heard.
When my brain's so fact-filled that it seems it will burst
Let my soul say, It's fine if you don't come in first.

I know I'll do well if I just concentrate—
For more isn't better by staying up late.
Whatever the grade, I know I am smart
If I live every moment and lead from the heart
And believe deep inside that I've done my best.
Whatever the outcome, I've passed my own test.

SELF-CONFIDENCE

I am not helpless
I am not weak
I will not shatter
I will not weep
I stand alone
Yet I stand strong
I can be me
Without being wrong

May I believe
That what I am
Is best for me
And not compare
Myself with others—
Friends or parents,
Sisters, brothers.

May I be proud
Of what I have,
My strengths and talents,
And not measure
Myself to others—
Friends or parents,
Sisters, brothers.

May I rejoice
In each distinction
That makes me special
And not compete
Against the others—
Friends or parents,
Sisters, brothers.

Let me tell myself
Today's tragedy
Is tomorrow's comedy,
And love is always.

Let me remind myself
Today's failure
Is tomorrow's victory,
And love is always.

Let me urge myself
Today's challenge
Is tomorrow's reward,
And love is always.

Let me forgive myself
Today's hurting
Is tomorrow's healing,
And love is always.

I pray I can spend just one single day
Without thinking "should" or "what if."
What freedom I'd have by living this way
Each moment, God's special gift!

I pray I can take all the guilt deep inside
And toss it away to the wind
And make all my choices with truth as my guide
By living "what is" from within.

May I have the courage it requires to say
What I want to do with my life today,
To stand up for all I desire for me,
To say that I'm old enough, now, to see.

May I have the passion to argue my views
With clear understanding so that I won't lose
My dreams and hopes for tomorrow as I go
Into the world with a self that I know.

Help me remember that patience
Is often rewarded with change,
That things that seem bad
Can turn good overnight,
That fate is incredibly strange.

Help me keep calm in a crisis,
Let me wait 'til the ultimate end,
For You give me strength
To live out my dreams
And turn enemies back into friends.

I have the talent to succeed
I have the direction to proceed
I have the knowledge to expand
I have the power to demand

I have the faith to seek and soar
I have the right to ask for more
I have the sense to know what's right
I have the strength to win the fight

I have the beauty to create
I have the empathy to relate
I have the energy to share
I have the love to show I care

May I change how I see my world,
Look past the dark to the bright,
Transform the ugly to beauty,
Exchange the shadows for light.

May I change how I see myself,
Look past all my anger to grace,
Transform every fear to courage,
Exchange all my boundaries for space.

Let my wild part remain
Untamed and running free—
Never chained,
Never reined,
Never sundered from me.

Let my wild part grow strong
Though it be safely hidden
From the eyes
Of the spies
Who say what is forbidden.

Let my wild part sing loud
The songs of generations.
Instinct found,
I am bound
To live by my creation.

GOD'S LOVE

What good does praying do?
What can I say?
When does God listen?
Once an hour? Once a day?
My soul speaks in silence,
My heart's like a stone.
How will God hear me
When I'm all alone?
But I will not doubt that
God knows what I feel.
Without words God answers—
Through love, prayers made real.

I pray that I can sleep tonight—
Put head to pillow, shut eyes tight,
Clear away each dreadful thought,
Replace with thanks for all I've got.
And as I meditate on Thee
I pray Your love descends on me
Until I feel that inner calm
That soothes me like a fragrant balm.

What was I before I was me?
A tulip, a queen, or a fish in the sea?
A beautiful leopard crouched in a tree?
What form did I take before I was me?

What was I twelve generations ago?
A pioneer woman, a horse, or a crow,
A painter, a doctor—I really don't know.
What form did I take generations ago?

What I do know is that each time I return
The form that I take is what I did earn.
My soul's progress grows the more that I learn
How to live in God's love each time I return.

In gloomy days and rainy nights
It seems my life is filled with gray,
And yet there is a source of light
Whenever I take time to pray.

When all seems dark and sure to break
I look within to find some hope,
And there You are to mend the ache,
To give me love so I can cope.

No matter what I write or draw
Or make from clay or decorate
It is myself, God's love inside,
That I express when I create.

For self-expression is my way
And self-truths mean I will not lose.
I know what makes creation real
When from within myself I choose.

There is always time to make a change
There is always space to turn around
There is always tomorrow to start again
There is always a new path to choose
There is always energy to move ahead
There is always light to guide the course
There is always God to show the way

Lord, grant me the eyes to see
the beauty of Your world.
Grant me the voice to speak
the words of Your prayers.
Grant me the strength to help
the children of Your creation.
Grant me the grace to feel
the joy of Your presence.
Grant me the insight to know
the peace of Your love.

Even though I'm still young, is there a way
For me to be totally centered each day?
Aware of my body, my mind, and my soul
Making choice after choice that keeps myself whole?

I know I'm not perfect, I'm no guru girl,
I can't stay so balanced when life's such a whirl.
I pray I can stop when I'm out of control,
Take a moment to tune out the urgent drumroll

For a quick whispered prayer that only I hear,
Is a gentle reminder that God is so near.
Then, I'm right back again to that calm, centered place
Where my body, my mind, and my soul are quite safe.

When my body aches to be held
And my soul reaches out for comfort,
Yet I'm all alone in a crowd of friends,
May I remember that God is with me.

When I want to speak but can't find the words
And if I could, there's no one to hear them,
Yet I long to share my innermost thoughts,
May I remember that God is listening.

When I've lost the path and cannot choose
And there's no one to show me the way,
Yet I must proceed for the time is short,
May I remember that God is guiding.

Getting Along
with
Family and Friends

Please, God, help me understand
Why grown-ups act the way they do—
As if they always see the way
And know exactly what to say,
When they are really quite confused
Or feel that they have been misused
But think pretending certainty
Is how to act in front of me.

Please, God, help me see beyond
The masks that grown-ups hide behind—
The laughing face that covers tears,
The scowling mouth that holds back fears—
For they forget how feelings count
And peek from all the masks they mount
To give me signals, cues, and signs
So I can read between their lines.

When my feelings are hurt by words that are mean,
When my heart wants to break and my head wants to
    scream,
May I look at the person who's speaking to me
And think beyond what I initially see
To what is really going on between us—
To what is the truth behind all of the fuss.

Because what's important is not who is right
Or what has been said in the midst of the fight,
But instead what I feel and what I can say
To help both of us find a more caring way.
And though I'm a child, let me pray to Above
To turn words used as weapons into words used as love.

What can I do when my friends turn their backs
And mock me and call me bad names?
What can I say when I walk down the hall
And I feel like my feet are in chains?

How can I smile when the tears are so near
And I bite my lips to keep calm?
Why is being me such a hard thing to do
And why am I weak and not strong?

Give me a song that my inner self sings
Or a prayer I can say on my own
About how the love that I have for myself
Keeps me safe through the day 'til I'm home.

I pray I'll choose friends who respect me,
Who treasure the girl that I am—
Who don't try to change,
Who don't rearrange
The person I'll be if I can.

I pray I'll choose friends who support me,
Who show me that they really care—
Who won't tear me down,
Who won't laugh or frown
When I ask them to help; they'll be there.

I pray I'll choose friends who'll grow with me,
Who'll walk the same path that I'm on—
Who like what I like,
Who fight the same fight,
Who will stay when the others have gone.

Sometimes the things that people say
Make me want to run away,
Make me want to hide someplace
And let the tears run down my face.

Sometimes the ways that people act
Make me want to hit them back,
Make me want to start a fight
Just to show them who is right.

Those times are the times I pray
That I can find a better way
To cope with what these people do,
For I have God to see me through.

Dear Lord, help me understand
What makes us fight,
What makes us snarl,
What makes us snipe,
What makes us circle round and round
Like wolves defending their own ground.

Dear Lord, help me understand
What makes us mean,
What makes us sharp,
What makes us scream,
What makes us find each other's faults
So that our anger somersaults.

Dear Lord, please help me find a way
To keep from fighting every day
At this young age, one truth I know:
Words said in anger are like a blow,
Like weapons aimed to pierce the heart
Each one tears our souls apart.

Then armed with understanding clear
I'll act from love instead of fear.

I need a friend to talk to
To share my hopes and fears.
I need a friend to be with
To share my jokes and tears.
I need a friend to give me
The honesty I seek,
To listen and to offer
Strength when I feel weak.

I'll give her all my secrets,
My love will know no bounds
I'll treat her as a sister,
A partner in life's rounds.
Our talks will be so precious
Yet never really end.
I'll not be truly happy
Until I have this friend.

May I believe this simple fact:
Perfection isn't where it's at.
Getting there is all the fun,
Not winning races but how they're run.

May this truth be like a light:
What I am is always right.
Pleasing others is joyless work
A part of me will always shirk.

May trying to be what I am not
Or hiding so I won't be caught
Be acts that I don't have to do.
To my own self I will be true.

I pray I will always be wise enough
To judge how people must see—
Not what they do or how they behave
And not what they say about me,

But how they are touched, deep down in their souls
By their fears, their pain, and their need.
If I am wise, then I will find out
That their view of themselves is the key.

When I look at someone on the street
Let me see God's child reflected back
And get beyond the differences—
Color, age, or how they're dressed—
Instead respect our common bond
Of two human beings sharing a moment
Here on earth.

When I talk to someone I've just met
Let me speak God's words with all I say
To get beyond the fear,
Break down the barriers between us
Of prejudice, language, and education
And build a bridge of understanding
In their place.

Let me have the self-control
To stop and think before I act,
To weigh my words before I speak,
To hold my peace and not fight back.

Let me take the time to choose
A way to handle confrontation
That lets the girl in me be guided
By my soul's communication.

Let me listen to higher spirits
When my anger binds me tight
Telling me to choose God's weapon,
Love will always win a fight.

Why do I have to be judged?
Why do I have to compete?
Why can't I just live
The life that I see
Instead of being what
People want me to be?

Why do I have to conform?
Why do I have to give in?
Why can't I just stand
Alone, not together
With those who destroy
The values I treasure?

Why do I have to achieve?
Why do I have to perform?
Why can't I just do
What my soul tells me I should,
As long as it's right,
As long as it's good?

My Blessings

What is a blessing, Lord?
How does it work?
Do you give it only when asked?
And is proof required—
Like on a math problem?
Do you pick and choose
Before I get
Your Seal of Approval
On my project?

What is a blessing, Lord?
How long does it last?
Can I keep one going forever?
Or must I repeat
The request every day
To show you I'm brave
About Your love,
About my faith,
About myself.

Thank you for dreams that take me to the places
I've only half thought of and never will see.
Soul-soaring adventures with secret companions
Each night offer insights to the essence of me.

Thank you for fantasies, so perfectly real,
My feelings transformed into pictures of old,
The voices of ancients from past generations
Telling the stories my soul longs to be told.

The song of my soul is mine for the singing
The answer of spirit is mine for the asking
The comfort of love is mine for the having
The joy of the heart is mine for the dancing
The peace of being is mine forever

Hip-hop, bebop, metal, rock and roll—
Thank you, God, for making music
That dances in my soul.
Let me take these joyous steps,
Forget myself in sound,
For only I can hear the songs
That twirl my heart around.
Blessed music makes me free,
It gives my spirit peace.
May I someday give back the gift
Of music for release.

Each morning may I wake anew
With all my voices sleeping still
So that my soul is what I hear
And not the shrill commands of will.

Each morning may I wake aware
Of all the blessings I can see—
How this day can be filled with joy
Because my world is inside me.

Each morning may I wake assured
That I have all the strength I need
To stop reacting to my fears
And let my Spirit take the lead.

Are You in heaven,
Looking down on us all,
Or are You deep inside,
Looking out through my eyes?
I need to believe
That You're here for the asking,
I need to be sure
That You'll help me survive.

I know there's no way
To ask for some proof,
I know that my faith
Is all there will be.
No voices, or visions,
Or angels' sweet songs—
All I have for believing
Is Your spirit in me.

It's the caress of the mist
And the sound of the wind
And the smell of the ocean nearby
That touches my soul,
That makes my heart yearn
'Til I wake in the night with a cry.

It's where sky meets the wave
And the wave licks the sand
And the sand holds the beach grasses tight
That heightens my pain,
That draws out my joy
'Til I run to the peace of the light.

Thank you, Lord, for this wonderful meal,
For the food and the drinks
And the way that I feel.
Thank you, Lord, for the people here
Who care about me
And whom I hold dear.
Thank you, Lord, for giving me more
Than I ever will need
When so many are poor.
Thank you, Lord, for loving me so,
Whatever I do,
Wherever I go.

ASKING FOR HELP

Talking to God is a natural thing,
It's like breathing
Or putting on shoes.
My soul feels the urge,
My mind finds the words,
And a prayer just happens
Like a whiff of smoke,
It rises from within
When no one else listens.

I need someone to listen
To what I did today,
For even though I'm not grown-up
I have a lot to say.

I need someone to take the time
To help me figure out
Just why I act the way I do
And what I'm all about.

But if that someone's busy
Or leaves me all alone,
Then let me talk to God instead,
For God is always home.

And as I tell God what I think
I'll start to gently hear
A song inside to comfort me—
God's loving voice so near.

I talk to myself all day—
Nothing profound.
Most of it is drivel,
Like what to do next.
But sometimes I pray.

I talk to myself all day—
My voices are boring,
I've heard them before.
They argue and bicker.
But sometimes I pray.

I talk to myself all day—
Should I do what they want
Or do what I want?
The question is always there.
But sometimes I pray.

I talk to myself all day—
Words so familiar
I'm tired of their sound.
So desperate for silence.
That's when I pray.

How do I know when You're listening to me?
Why should I trust that You care?
What can I see when I look at my world
That proves You will always be there?

How do I feel Your protection?
Where can I go that You're near?
What can I pray that will bring You inside
When I'm helpless and shivering with fear?

The answers are all in the knowing
That I have Your love most of all
And it never matters what happens
You'll always be there when I fall.

Just as the sun shines through the mist
My prayer lights a path through my pain
So I can connect my mind with my soul
And travel to God once again.

Just as the ocean returns with the tide
My prayer is a way to regain
My trust and my faith in God's loving plan
That there is a reason I came.

I pray I'll be calm in the storm
I pray I'll keep cool in the fray
I pray I'll perform in the crunch
I pray I'll stay strong through the day
I pray I'll have courage to choose
I pray I'll use faith to decide
I pray I'll make right what is wrong
I pray I'll let love be my guide
I pray I'll get out of myself
I pray I'll stand bravely and tall
I pray I'll speak truth and not lies
I pray I'll be generous to all

Sometimes I don't believe my prayers,
I say them out of habit.
The prayers are simply one more way
To greet the night and end the day.

Sometimes I don't believe my prayers,
I don't make the connection
Between my heart and what I feel
And how my words describe what's real.

Sometimes I don't believe my prayers,
And yet I'm glad I pray,
For when I need to believe a prayer
The way to say it will be there.

If I talk to you, Lord, all through the day,
Do You feel what I feel when You hear what I say?
If I pray for the insight and You make my soul see,
Do You hope that I'll thank You for being there for me?
And if I get angry because I can't find
Your answers to prayers that I make in my mind—
So doubting Your Presence, I begin to replace
Your love everlasting with doubts that disgrace—
Do You weep for my weakness, my failures, my pain?
Or wait, knowing soon I will trust once again.

My prayers are like water that quenches
When my throat is dry and hot.
My soul's calling to higher voices:
Help me, hear me, calm me, love me,
I'm just a girl with words.

My prayers are like food that fills me
When my body is tired and hungry.
My soul's calling to higher spirits:
Touch me, hold me, soothe me, keep me
Safe with you.

Why do I find it so hard to pray?
Why are there suddenly no words to say?
As if all my prayers are blocked deep inside
And if I tried praying, God would know I had lied.

Why do I find it so hard to pray
When talking to God is part of my day?
I try to think thoughts that are gentle and kind
To ask for a blessing, but they've flown from my mind.

Why do I find it so hard to pray?
Perhaps I should stop saying "give me" and "may"
And instead just give in to my soul's silent song,
Trusting and knowing my prayers haven't gone.

Tell me, God, where do I go?
Where do I fit?
When will I know?

Tell me, God, what must I be?
How can I act
And be true to me?

Tell me, God, what do I say,
What words do I use
To express my own way?

Listen, child, to your own heart:
Follow your feelings,
You'll know your part.

Listen, child, to your own voice:
You'll find the path
To your soul's choice.

Listen, child, trust what you hear:
The answers are in you,
There's nothing to fear.

Give me the wisdom to find moments to pray
Each morning or evening or times through the day,
Even at school when a teacher drones on
Or at lunchtime or hall time when everyone's gone.

Give me the courage to reach down inside
To ask for the guidance I need to survive,
To treasure the question as a sign I'm just fine
And know that the answer will be there in time.

Prayers can be stated, shouted, or sung,
Drummed and doodled or danced until done,
Whispered, whimpered, waved like a flag,
Pleaded, promised, put in a bag,
Chanted, chosen, chewed on like gum,
Looked at, laughed at, learned on the run.

Prayers can be written, wrapped up and sent,
Crayoned, chalked, or collected like rent,
Folded, faxed, found hidden in halls,
Painted, plastered, pinned up on walls,
Sculpted, scrambled, scripted in gold—
There's never a way a prayer can get old.

Like mist softly shrouding the shore
The sadness rolls over my soul
And I wait stopped in time
For the prayer that is mine
To shine through this fog to my core

Like the sand taken back by the tide
I'm lost in a life unfulfilled
And I pray for relief
In reluctant belief
That I'll turn to find God by my side

FEARLESS FAITH

May I forgive myself each day
For things I do, for things I say
That make me feel ashamed inside
As if some part of me has died.
And let me always know the truth
That God's light shines upon my youth
And young girls such as I are blessed
With goodness underneath the rest
And deep down there is love to find
To make tomorrow's acts more kind.

Let me forget my yesterday life—
It's done, it's finished, it's through.
And if I get worried about tomorrow,
The truth is, I haven't a clue.

But if I stop searching for answers,
I'll find that today is the key,
For living the moment is all that there is
And joy is the Spirit in me.

Help me, Lord, to guard my dreams,
Precious jewels inside my soul,
Treasures no one else can know,
Seeds from which my life will grow.

Help me, Lord, to keep dreams safe,
Sheltered from the world of facts,
Hidden from harsh grown-up light
That judges what is true and right.

Help me, Lord, to hold dreams close,
Protect my most fantastic joys
Against all those who say I'm wrong
To hear imagination's song.

Please, God, help me mend myself:
The little pieces chipped away
From hearing other people say
"Don't try"
"You'll fail"
"Can't risk"
"No way."

Please, God, help me heal myself:
The wounds I've taken in my fight
Against those who presume they're right—
Put down,
Betrayed,
Lied to,
Bound tight.

Please, God, help me keep myself
Protected from being pulled apart
By words designed to break my heart:
"Pretend"
"Act nice"
"Keep quiet"
"Not smart."

I know with some faith I'll find a good way
To untangle the feelings that fill up my day.
The tightest of knots preserves all my fears,
The ends are quite hidden and slippery with tears.
I'm certain my parents tied bows that would last
To hide the mistakes that they made in my past.
Yet I am still young and have courage besides,
All I need is one loop to unravel their lies—
A strand gently straightened leading backwards in time
To the love and forgiveness originally mine.

Let me grab a star
And pull it toward me
Along with the sky,
A blanket of wishes
To keep hope warm
Woven softly with moonlight
To cover my dreams.

There's a voice deep inside me,
A loud insistent call
That talks and talks the whole day through
And worries about it all.

Sometimes it blames me for the things
I've done that may be bad,
Sometimes it whispers scary threats
That make me feel quite sad.

Please help me, God, to tell my voice
To stop this talk of blame
And let the other voices speak,
The ones that bring no shame.

These voices sing a hopeful song
That makes my spirit soar.
Please help me, God, to find a way
To listen to them more.

May I have the faith
To dare the impossible.
May I have the courage
To do more than I can.
May I have the wisdom
To handle my failures.
May I have the strength
To bend and not break.

Please help me to choose
When the choosing is hard,
When each choice makes such sense
I could go either way
It depends on a whim,
It's not easy to say.

Please help me decide
When deciding is tough,
When right blends into wrong
And the arguments smear,
When there's lots of confusion
And the path isn't clear.

Please help me to learn,
Though the learning may hurt,
Not to run from the task
But to choose and then live
For the choice that I make
Shows how much I can give.

May I have faith that I can do it,
May I keep my spirit strong,
Ignoring those who laugh at me—
For I will prove them wrong.

May I know what I am made of,
May I trust I'll overcome
The odds stacked high against me—
Tomorrow I'll have won.

May I cherish every inner hope,
May I nourish every dream
That takes me down the path I make—
I'm more than what I seem.

There's a quiet place deep within
Where my self lives and listens in.
She helps me know just how I feel
And how to laugh at what's not real.
She goes and gets the thoughts I need—
When Better Self has space to lead
She whispers secrets that are true
And stories to tell me what to do.
She's like a little child, but strong,
A guide to follow all life long.
And in those moments filled with light
It's my child soaring in joyful flight.

When someone dies whom I once loved
I pray her angel from above
Returns awhile to comfort me
And deep within my heart can see
How much I tried, how much I cared
About those times we laughed and shared.
And one day, with our separate souls
Not trapped by distance, time, and roles,
I hope that I will feel the touch
Of someone whom I loved so much.

LIVING IN
THE MOMENT

I pray that I'll reach out
To find in each day
One single moment
Perfected in time.
That I'll stop and take notice
Of God's world around me—
The brilliant green grass
Glowing in sunlight,
The smell of the lilacs,
The touch of warm air—
All nature's creations
Filling my spirit,
Making me whole,
Giving me hope.

The night that I was born, as the clock struck seven
I came into this world, a gift from heaven.
And all the nurses laughed, for my face was smiling
To be here on this earth and to be so beguiling.
They say I had dimples where the angels kissed me
As tokens of their love and to show they'd miss me.
And I was blessed with life, a new soul parting
The night that I was born, purest love just starting.

Let me capture this moment
Of happiness
And keep it
Wrapped up inside me
Like a secret
Until tomorrow
When I wake
To open it,
A present to my soul.

I pray I keep with me this moment of glory
When the light shines clear
And the wind is still,
When the sky offers hope
And the world holds its breath
Waiting for me to take notice.

I pray I keep with me this moment of glory
When I have grown older
And girlhood has gone.
When my soul cries out
May this moment remain
Waiting for me to take notice.

Help me remember that moment of happiness
When I was a child
And my world was a garden,
When I picked wild strawberries alone in the sunlight,
Knowing somehow that my time there was precious.

Help me remember that moment of happiness
When the air stood still
And I walked in grace,
When my heart was dancing and my soul was one
With the beauty around me and the love inside.

On the shortest day of the year
May I know how sweet is the light
As it shines on the paths I follow
And reflects on each choice that is right.

Let the light lead me into the evening
As dusk falls early and long,
When it's only a candle's brief flicker
Illuminating right from wrong.

May I live in the moment,
May I breathe in the day.
Let my heart fill with joy,
Greet the dawn's early ray.

Let me make my hours timeless,
Let me never forget
That the past is behind me
And tomorrow's not yet.

May I smile with the knowledge
That now is the best.
Let me love where I am
And laugh at the rest.

Making
a Difference

Let me share
My innocence,
My joyfulness,
My smile
With someone who
Has lost the chance
To visit with a child.

Let me give
My gentle touch,
My laugh,
My whole embrace
To someone who
Would wait all day
To gaze into my face.

Let me help someone today,
Lend a hand or give away
Time I usually spend in play.

Let me leave something today
With someone who will never say
A word of thanks or gift repay.

Let me go somewhere today
Guided by the words I pray
To offer love in my own way.

What can I give to this world today
That returns a little of what I take,
That shows that I'm able, because I am me,
To help other people through choices I make?

What can I do for this world today
That makes it better than when the sun rose,
Something I do that wasn't demanded,
Or even better, something nobody knows?

What can I say to this world today
That someone will hear and feel good,
Words from the heart and not from the head
Expressing my love as no other words could?

Let me be generous with my talents,
Let me be giving of my mind,
Let me lend help when it is needed,
Let me offer others my time.

May I hold the hand of the lonely,
May I portion my wealth to the poor,
May I share what I eat with the hungry,
As I get, may I give even more.

For I am blessed with good fortune,
My angels smile often on me.
May I never ignore those less gifted,
Less happy, less cherished, less free.

I pray that the person I am becoming
Is someone who'll give to the world
A little more courage, a little more grace,
An example to follow, a more caring face.

I pray that the knowledge I'm getting
Will someday help people to know
A little more love, a little more faith,
Something I'll leave for the whole human race.

I pray that the Spirit I'm blessed with
Will guide me on my special path,
A little more sure, a little more clear,
So others will follow without any fear.

I'm not too young to begin to see
The mission life has given me.
Although the goals are far away
May I get glimpses every day
So I can keep my joy alive,
So that my purpose will survive,
So that one day I'll be prepared
To say to all that I have dared
To make this world a better place,
To make my mark, to leave my trace.

WHEN I'M ALONE

When I'm hurried through life
From the moment I wake,
Rushed from home right to school,
Told there's no time to take,

When I'm bundled like groceries
And carted around,
Fulfilling a schedule
That's getting me down,

When fun becomes offered
As an in-between treat
And everyone's screaming
About deadlines to meet,

Then let me find peace
In a place without stress,
A place deep inside me,
A place I can rest.

I need someone to comfort me,
To tell me it's okay,
To stroke my hair
And kiss my cheek,
To hold me tight when I feel weak,
To make hurt go away.

I need someone to care for me,
Someone who's always there
To take my hand
And wipe my tears,
To stand on guard against my fears,
To help when life's unfair.

I trust in God's great love for me
When I am all alone
To hear my cry
And fill my heart
With faith that I can do my part
And manage on my own.

Sometimes it's hard to find a place
To be alone without disgrace,
A place where I can cry and scream
Or simply close my eyes and dream,
A place where no one comes to see
What I am doing or if I'm free.
Sometimes it's hard to find a spot
To be myself and not be caught,
As though to be alone is bad,
A sign I'm fearful, sick, or sad.
What they don't see and I can't say
Is that being alone is a time to pray.

May I find God in drops of rain
That fall across my windowpane
On a bleak December day.

May I find God in eyes I see
Glaring back in the mirror at me
When I don't get my way.

May I find God in the lowliest task
That anyone could ever ask
A person to do.

May I find God in that ugly place
Where my conscience goes when I must face
That I have lied and been untrue.

May I find God in everything
And every person I will be—
For God is everywhere in me.

When I'm feeling afraid and unsure
Because life's overwhelming and shrill,
When there's homework and walking the dog
And also a basketball drill,
When I worry all day that I'll fail
Because there's so much I must do
And I find myself almost in tears
Because I'm one girl and not two,
Then I need to go back to that place
Where I'm calm—deep inside me.
Lead me, God, back to the path.

Sometimes I feel I'm so alone,
As if there's no one else but me.
I'm separated from my friends
By feelings no one else can see.

Sometimes I think I've built a wall
To keep me hidden from the crowd,
A wall of words I cannot say
And thoughts I can't express out loud.

And then I know that only You
Can hear my softly whispered plea
For just one friend whom I can trust
Enough to share what's inside me.

Help me fill my loving cup
From deep inside myself.
Help me take the unmet need
Down from the waiting shelf
And search my own emotions
To find a way to help.

Help me answer all my prayers
With words from my own heart.
Help me mend my lovely dreams
The world has torn apart
And see within my purpose here
A place where I can start.

Arms reaching
Palms lifting
Feet wandering
Mind questioning
Heart awakening
Soul opening
Spirit evolving . . .
An endless search

Body maturing
Emotions exploding
Confidences growing
Tastes changing
Faith strengthening
Vision expanding
Love deepening . . .
On life's cusp

PRAYERS FOR MY SELF

CELIA STRAUS is a writer for print, film, and video. Her scripts have garnered over 150 top professional awards. She is a graduate of Mary Washington College of the University of Virginia, and earned an M.A. in English literature from Georgetown University. She has taught English and drama to high school and college students. She lives in Washington, D.C., with her husband and two daughters.

If you would like to contact Celia directly or would like a prayer written just for you, visit her Web site at www.girlprayers.com.